W9-AKE-805

429-9575

An I Can Read Book®

THE MIXED-UP GRANDMAS TREASURY

Three books by Emily Arnold McCully

BARNES
&NOBLE
B O O K S
N E W   Y O R K

ISBN 0–7607–0743-X

CONTENTS

. . . .

For Penny MacDonald and Em Brinkley

An I Can Read Book®

The Grandma Mix-up

**Story and Pictures by
Emily Arnold McCully**

HarperTrophy
A Division of HarperCollins*Publishers*

CONTENTS

1 THE MIX-UP

Pip's mom and dad
were taking a trip.

"We will be gone
two days and two nights,"
said Pip's mom.
"Grandma Nan
will take care of you."

Mom and Dad and Pip

went downstairs

to wait for Grandma Nan.

9

"Here she comes!" cried Pip.

"Hi, Grandma Nan!"

"Hello, hello," said Grandma Nan.

"How is my good grandchild?"

Just then

a taxi raced up.

Out popped Grandma Sal.

"Here I am," she called.

"Did you ask Grandma Sal to baby-sit?"

Mom asked Dad.

"Did you ask Grandma Nan to baby-sit?"

Dad asked Mom.

"Now what will we do?"

"No matter," said Grandma Sal.

"We can both baby-sit!"

"Are you sure?" asked Dad.

"Run along," said Grandma Sal.

"We will have a fine time."

"Good-bye, Pip," said Dad.

"We will miss you," said Mom.

16

They hugged Pip good-bye
and rode away in a taxi.

2 A BAD START

"Well!" said Grandma Nan.

"Let's get busy!"

"Let's relax!"

said Grandma Sal.

"Open your treat bag, Pip."

"Gummy Bears," said Pip.

"Thank you!"

"Come upstairs,"

said Grandma Nan.

"First thing in the morning,

I inspect your room."

20

Pip followed her upstairs.

"Oh, Pip," said Grandma Nan sadly.

"Our room is a mess!

We must clean it up!"

Pip put away the socks
and trucks and crayons,
and pulled up the bed covers.
Grandma Nan was very strict!

"Pip, Pip!" called Grandma Sal

from the backyard.

"Come down

and show me your bike!"

Pip ran outside.

"Look at you!"

said Grandma Sal.

"You are a super-duper rider!"

"Hi-ho," called Grandma Nan.

"It is noon on the dot.

Time to eat lunch."

Pip and Grandma Sal went inside.

"You may have tuna with sprouts,"

said Grandma Nan.

26

"Or an apple, some nuts,

a marshmallow, cereal, pretzels,

or corned-beef hash,"

said Grandma Sal.

It was too hard to choose.

"I'm not hungry," Pip said.

"Oh, dear. I don't like

the sound of that,"

said Grandma Nan.

"Maybe a nap is in order."

28

"You bet your life!"

said Grandma Sal.

She plopped down

onto the couch.

"See you later, Pip."

3 WORSE AND WORSE

"Rise and shine!"

called Grandma Nan.

"Nap time is over.

We want to be busy now!"

"What do we want to do?"

asked Pip.

"Oh, paint us a picture,"

said Grandma Nan.

"Or act out a story...

or do a puzzle...."

31

Grandma Sal was in the living room

"The big game is on TV,"

she said.

"Want to watch?

Want a chip?"

"I think I will go

back upstairs," said Pip.

Pip sat down

to write a secret letter.

"Dear Mom and Dad,

Grandma Nan is too hard,

and Grandma Sal is too easy.

I want you to come home

and do things our way.

Love, Pip."

Pip put the letter
into the desk drawer
and went out front
to sit on the steps.

"Dinner time!"

called Grandma Nan.

"Please set the table."

37

Grandma Nan was stirring a big pot.

"Stew!" she said.

"If it stinks," said Grandma Sal,

"we can send out for pizza."

Pip ate one bite of stew

to be polite.

"Pip," said Grandma Nan,

"we must eat to be strong."

"Now, Nan," said Grandma Sal,

"the child will not starve."

"May I go outside?"

asked Pip.

"If you keep clean,"

said Grandma Nan.

40

"Pip can always take a bath,"

said Grandma Sal.

Both grandmas were grumpy.

4 DOING THINGS PIP'S WAY

Pip went outside

to swing high on the swing.

Grandma Nan wanted

to do things one way,

and Grandma Sal wanted

to do things another way.

Pip wanted to do things

the way Mom and Dad and Pip

always did them.

The grandmas were talking

by the window.

"A child needs rules, Sal,"

said Grandma Nan.

"A child needs fun, Nan,"

said Grandma Sal.

"My rule is bed at 8 o'clock,"

said Grandma Nan.

"Oh, loosen up,"

said Grandma Sal.

"A body gets

the sleep it needs."

"STOP!" cried Pip.

"I do not want

to do everything two ways.

I want to do them *our* way,

like every day

when Mom and Dad are home."

"How is that, dear?"

asked Grandma Nan.

"I clean up my room
once a week.
I make my own lunch
every day.
I don't take a nap
unless I want to,
and I never have candy
in the morning
except at Christmas.
No TV on nice days,
and I can get dirty when I play.
And I don't eat vegetables
all mixed up with meat."

"What do you think, Sal?"
asked Grandma Nan.
"The child has a point,"
said Grandma Sal.

"Pip, we will try

to do things your way,"

said Grandma Nan.

"How do we begin?"

"It is almost my bedtime,"
said Pip.

"But first
I put on my pajamas,
and then I brush my teeth
and pet kitty
and wash my face.
Then I look out for stars
and eat a cookie
and run my trucks,
and then I bounce on my bed
if I feel like it.
Then you can read me a story."

"Oh, goody, a story,"

said Grandma Nan.

She reached for the bookshelf.

"Oh, goody," said Grandma Sal.

She reached into her bag.

"Oh, no," said Pip.

"*I* choose the book.

It is upstairs.

You can take turns reading it."

Pip got ready for bed.

The grandmas waited.

After a while,

Grandma Nan called up,

"It's getting late, Pip!"

"Relax, Nan," said Grandma Sal.

The grandmas laughed.

Finally

Pip crawled under the covers.

Then Grandma Nan

read the first page,

and Grandma Sal

read the next page

of Pip's bedtime book.

They took turns

to the very end.

After that,

the grandmas

did almost everything

Pip's way—

until Pip's mom and dad

came home.

GRANDMAS
AT THE LAKE

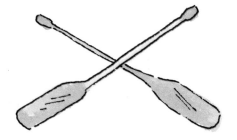

An I Can Read Book®

GRANDMAS AT THE LAKE

story and pictures by
Emily Arnold McCully

HarperTrophy
A Division of HarperCollinsPublishers

For Raya, and B.G.,

and three generations of sailors

One hot summer day

Grandma Nan telephoned.

"I have rented a cabin at the lake,"

she said.

"I have invited Grandma Sal.

We would like Pip to visit too."

Grandma Sal said,

"Tell Pip to bring a friend.

The more the merrier."

"Tell them to be good,"

said Grandma Nan.

"Oh, Nan," said Grandma Sal.

Pip asked Ski to come along.

"We can swim and hike and row,

and have a great time!" said Pip.

"I can't wait!" said Ski.

When they got to the lake,

Ski shouted, "Last one in

is a rotten egg!"

10

"Hold on there,"

said Grandma Nan.

"First you unpack."

"Throw your stuff anyplace,"

said Grandma Sal.

12

"Not so fast," said Grandma Nan.

"Underwear goes in this drawer.

Shirts and shorts go in this one."

"Whatever," said Grandma Sal.

"Now may we swim?" asked Pip.

"Why not?" said Grandma Sal.

14

"First we eat lunch,"

said Grandma Nan.

"Then we wait one hour.

Then we swim."

15

Grandma Nan made

tuna and sprout sandwiches.

Grandma Sal opened a bag of cookies.

"No cookies

until you eat your sandwiches,"

said Grandma Nan.

"What's the difference?"

said Grandma Sal.

"They will end up together anyway."

16

Everyone waited exactly one hour.

Then Pip and Ski put on

their bathing suits.

So did Grandma Nan.

"Oh, no," said Ski.

"Is she coming too?"

"Dip time!" called Grandma Sal.

"Oh, no," said Ski.

"Stay inside the ropes,"

said Grandma Nan.

"No splashing!"

"Relax, Nan," said Grandma Sal.

"It's only water."

Pip and Ski dove.

"Where are the children?"

cried Grandma Nan.

She blew and blew her whistle.

Pip and Ski came up for air.

"Take it easy, Nan,"

said Grandma Sal.

"You have upset the fish."

Grandma Nan swam ten laps.

Then she blew her whistle again.

"Time to dry off!" she called.

"But we are not ready!" said Pip.

"You do not want to catch a chill,"
said Grandma Nan.

"A chill?" said Grandma Sal.

"The sun is hot as blazes!"

25

Grandma Nan led them back

to the cabin.

"Pip," said Ski, "these grandmas

will drive me nuts.

If one says yes,

the other says no."

"Let's get away from them,"

said Pip.

"How about playing in the woods?"

"Right!" said Ski.

"Let's go play in the woods!"

"Ski and I are going for a walk,"
said Pip.

"Great!" said Grandma Nan.

"We will take a nature hike."

"But we want to be alone!" said Pip.

"Nonsense!" said Grandma Nan.

"You cannot have fun alone!"
said Grandma Sal.

"We will write down what we see
in this nature notebook,"
said Grandma Nan.

"How about cookies for the hike?"

asked Grandma Sal.

"No. Dried fruit and sunflower seeds

are good for a hike,"

said Grandma Nan.

"Oh, no," said Pip.

"Our plan has failed."

"We have to think of another one,"

said Ski.

31

They followed a path into the woods.

"Hark!" said Grandma Nan.

"Is that the song

of the tufted titmouse?"

"Search me," said Grandma Sal.

"Let's sing along, kids.

Merrily we roll along, roll along..."

'You have scared away the titmouse,"

aid Grandma Nan.

"Let's have our snacks,"

said Grandma Sal.

Grandma Nan got out the dried fruit

and sunflower seeds.

"This is for the birds,"

said Grandma Sal.

"Good idea," said Grandma Nan.

"We will feed the birds."

Pip and Ski scattered some seeds.

"We will never have any fun,"

said Ski.

"We will think of a way," said Pip.

"Let us clean up our campsite,"

said Grandma Nan.

"It is time to go home."

"Who wants a nap?"

asked Grandma Sal.

She plopped down on her bed.

Grandma Nan yawned.

"I am worn out," she said.

"Lie down, Pip and Ski," she said.

Soon the grandmas were asleep.

Pip and Ski heard them snore.

"This is our chance!" said Pip.

"Let's go!" said Ski.

They tiptoed to the door.

Slowly, they opened it.

Creak, creak.

"Where to?" asked Ski.

"To the middle of the lake!" said Pip.

"They can't bother us there!"

"Grandma Nan might get mad,"

said Ski.

"Grandma Sal would want

to come too,"

said Pip.

Just then they heard

"YOO-HOO!"

"Oh, no," said Pip.

"Here they come!"

Pip untied the boat.

Ski jumped in and sat down.

Pip jumped in and shoved off.

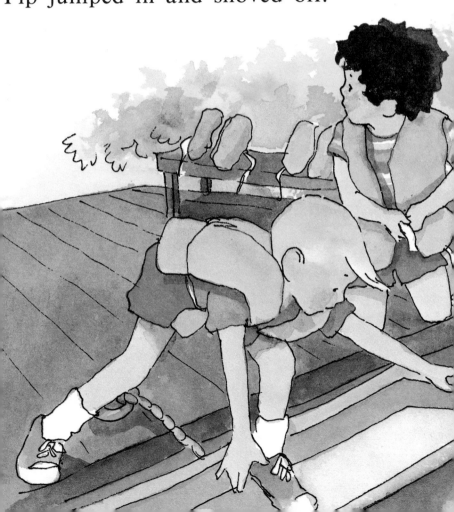

"EEEEEK!" cried Grandma Nan.

"Come back, come back!"

"We are just taking

a little ride," said Pip.

Pip and Ski watched Grandma Nan get smaller and smaller.

Grandma Sal ran to the dock.

"Pip and Ski are lost at sea!"

cried Grandma Nan.

"How could they leave

without us?" said Grandma Sal.

The boat turned in circles.

"We have to row together," said Pip.

They tried again.

The boat moved in a straight line.

Grandma Nan and Grandma Sal

got even smaller.

"This all happened

because I took a nap!"

cried Grandma Nan.

A crowd gathered on the dock.

Everyone waved at the boat.

"Those kids are good sailors,"

said Grandma Sal.

"And they are wearing

their life preservers."

"Let's row to that island," said Pip.

"Okay," said Ski.

"We had better go back now," said Pip.

"The grandmas will be worried."

They rowed and rowed
toward the dock.

"Pip! Ski!" called Grandma Nan.

"Please come back!"

"We will if you make us a promise,"
said Pip.

"What do you mean?"
asked Grandma Nan.

Pip said,

"I mean Grandma Nan says one thing
and Grandma Sal says another.
You never let us say what we want."

"Pip has a point," said Grandma Sal.

"What do you want us to promise?"

"Promise to let us have fun!" said Pip.

"Promise to let us play

by ourselves," said Ski.

"Sal?" asked Grandma Nan.

"Okay by me," said Grandma Sal.

"We promise!" called the grandmas.

"Thank you!" said Pip and Ski.

They rowed up to the dock.

"Will you come for a ride?"

asked Pip.

"Well," said Grandma Nan.

"We would love to!"

said Grandma Sal.

Grandma Nan sat in the stern.

Grandma Sal sat in the bow.

Pip and Ski rowed back

to the middle of the lake.

"Kids," said Grandma Sal,

"you run a tight ship!"

"Relax and enjoy the ride," said Ski.

They rowed past the island.

"This is very nice,"

said Grandma Nan.

"But Ski needs to pull more

on his oar."

"Don't rock the boat, Nan,"

said Grandma Sal.

GRANDMAS AT BAT

GRANDMAS AT BAT

By Emily Arnold McCully

HarperTrophy
A Division of HarperCollins*Publishers*

To Sam Jones

Contents

No Coach

"Our coach has chicken pox!"

said Pip,

"and our first game is on Saturday!"

"What a shame," said Mom.

"They will not let us play

if we cannot find a new coach,"

said Pip.

"I love baseball,"

said Grandma Sal.

"I could be your coach."

"Oh, Sal," said Grandma Nan,

"you don't know what a coach does."

"Yes I do," said Grandma Sal.

"I watch the games on TV."

"Watching is not doing,"

said Grandma Nan.

"I have played baseball.

I will help."

"I didn't know you played baseball,"

said Grandma Sal.

"You don't know lots of things,"

said Grandma Nan.

The telephone rang.

It was Ski.

"Bad news," he said.

"We can't find a coach.

The game will be called off."

"Maybe it won't," said Pip.

"I have two coaches right here."

"Who?" asked Ski.

"Grandma Nan and Grandma Sal,"

said Pip.

"Your *grandmas*?" cried Ski.

"Pip, we have a big game

on Saturday!"

12

"So we will practice," said Pip,

"and the grandmas can watch."

"But you know your grandmas . . ."

said Ski.

"As long as we can play," said Pip,

"who cares who is coach?"

Practice

"Yoo-hoo, Stings,"

called Grandma Sal.

"How do you do, team,"

said Grandma Nan.

"This is Dolores, Julio, Aggie,

14

Mona, Tad, Grace, Norman,

and you know Ski," said Pip.

"What a big team!" said Grandma Sal.

"It's nine players, Sal,"

said Grandma Nan.

"That is a baseball team!"

15

"Time for warm-up exercises!"

said Grandma Nan.

"Come on, Sal, show the team!"

"You first, Nan," said Grandma Sal.

"Show them how you do push-ups."

"Grandmas," said Pip,

"we know what to do.

We need to practice playing."

"Okay," said Grandma Sal.

"Hold up that glove, Nan.

Watch how I throw," said Grandma Sal.

"Oops!"

"Sal, they should practice batting.

You are up first," said Grandma Nan.

"Nan, you are a bossy boots!"

said Grandma Sal.

"I am the coach!" said Grandma Nan.

"Coaches give orders."

"Not to other coaches,"

said Grandma Sal.

20

"Do something, Pip," said Ski.

"Your grandmas are

driving us bananas!"

"Grandmas, stop!" cried Pip.

"Okay," said Grandma Nan.

"I will hit first."

21

"Sal, I can't hit your pitches,"

said Grandma Nan.

"It takes a while to warm up,"

said Grandma Sal.

CRAAACK!

'Wow," said Grandma Sal. "Run, Nan!"

"The coaches are hogging the field!"

cried Grace.

"Grandmas!" Pip yelled.

"*We* need to practice playing!

Please sit on the bench and watch!"

"Just watch?" said Grandma Sal.

"Not coach?" said Grandma Nan.

"We all *know* what to do!" said Pip.

"You do?" asked Grandma Sal.

"Of course!" said Pip.

"All right," said Grandma Nan.

"Go and play," said Grandma Sal.

"Hooray!" cried the Stings.

The grandmas watched.

"These kids are good,"

said Grandma Sal.

"They don't need us,"

said Grandma Nan.

28

"I feel left out," said Grandma Sal.

"I do too," said Grandma Nan.

"You know, Nan," said Grandma Sal,

"I think I know a way we can help!"

"Oh, Sal," said Grandma Nan,

"I think I know too!"

The Game

It was Saturday.

The Stings were waiting

to play the Grubs.

"Where are the grandmas?"

asked Ski.

"I don't know," said Pip,

"but I know they will come."

"I hope they don't do

anything funny," said Aggie.

"They won't," Pip said,

and crossed her fingers.

"Yoo-hoo!"

"Grandmas!" cried Pip.

"Uh-oh," said Mona.

"They look weird!"

"You can just watch us play, okay?"

said Pip.

"Don't worry about us, Pip,"

said Grandma Nan.

"Batter up!" called the umpire.

The Grubs were first at bat.

Pip pitched.

Three Grubs got base hits.

Ski went to the mound

to talk to Pip.

"What is the matter?" he asked.

"It's my grandmas," Pip said.

"They look so silly."

"Just think about pitching,"

said Ski.

But the next Grub hit a double,

and another Grub hit a home run.

Then a Grub hit a pop fly,

and Aggie caught the ball.

Ski made a double play.

The score was now Grubs 5, Stings 0.

It was the Stings' turn to bat.

Dolores hit a long drive,

but it was caught.

Aggie hit a fly to third base.

Pip struck out.

In the sixth inning

the score was Grubs 6, Stings 0.

"This is hopeless," said Julio.

"We cannot get a hit."

"Nan, this is not good,"

said Grandma Sal.

"The team needs us now!"

said Grandma Nan.

"That's right!" said Grandma Sal.

"Let's go!"

Grandmas Go to Bat

It was the last inning.

The grandmas jumped off the bench.

44

"Rah team rah!" they cheered.

"Sis boom bah!"

"Oh no," said Pip.

"Not now, Grandmas," said Ski.

45

"The ball has wings

when it's hit by Stings!"

the grandmas shouted.

"Put the Stings to the test;

they are the best!"

46

"They think we're the best,"

said Dolores.

47

"On the mound,

on the bases,

in the field,

Stings are aces!"

cried the grandmas.

They shook their pom-poms.

"Maybe we *can* win,"

said Norman.

"Shake them up,

shake them up!"

the grandmas yelled.

"You can do it, Stings,"

called the crowd.

"Huzza huzza,

pow pow pow!

Sting them, sting them,

now now now!"

shouted the grandmas.

"Hear that, team?" said Pip.

"Let's win it for the grandmas!"

"All right!" yelled the Stings.

"Strike them out!"

yelled Grandma Sal.

"You can do it!"

52

Pip struck out three Grubs.

When the Stings went to bat,

Mona hit a single.

"More hits," cried the grandmas.

Ski hit a double.

Tad hit a home run.

"We're not quitters;

we're home-run hitters!"

the grandmas shouted.

56

Grace hit another home run.

Then Julio hit a triple,

Dolores hit a double,

and Mona hit a home run.

The score was Stings 7, Grubs 6.

The Stings had won!

"We won it for the grandmas,"

said Ski.

"You won it because

you are the Stings,"

said Grandma Sal,

"and the Stings are the best."

"Thanks, Grandmas," said Pip.

"You are welcome,"

said Grandma Nan.

"Well, Sal, I will never forget today.

It was fun being a cheerleader."

"Grandmas," said Pip,

"we want you to cheer

at every game we play."

"Oh my," said Grandma Sal.

62

"What do you think, Nan?"

"I think we need new pom-poms,"

said Grandma Nan.

"These are worn out!"

Then the Stings yelled,

"On the field

and at the plate,

who makes sure

the Stings are great?

Grandmas, Grandmas,

Grandmas, YAY!"